ALL COTTON BRIEFS

ALL COTTON BRIEFS

EXPANDED EDITION

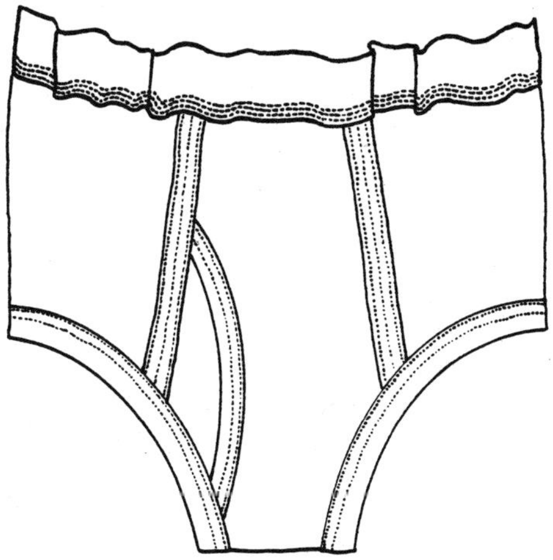

M. KASPER

BENZENE
BROOKLYN

ISBN : 0-939194-05-8

Published by

BENZENE
BROOKLYN

Underwritten by a grant from

XERIC
FOUNDATION

Distributed by

LEFT LANE MUST TURN LEFT

106 HIGH ST. FLORENCE MASS. 01060

"All Cotton Briefs ~ Expanded Edition" is a revised, enlarged version of "All Cotton Briefs", published in 1985, in Iowa, by The North American Review. That was a revised version of "20 Trial Briefs", published in 1981, in California, by The Fault Press.

Some of these pieces appeared in
Ambit, 11×30, The Fault, Fifth Estate,
Gui, Lost and Found Times,
The Minnesota Review,
The North American Review,
The Northampton Herald,
Not Guilty!, Oink!, Only Paper Today,
OR, Scat, Scree, Strange Faeces, Stony Hills,
Titmouse Review, and the Wormwood Review.

Special thanks to Peter Cherches and Robley Wilson

CONTENTS.

BY THE 1450'S FEW COULD AFFORD THE CLOTHES ADVERTISED IN THE PAINTINGS OF MEMLING & VAN EYCK

The phrase 'to fleece someone' originated as follows:

In 1279, precisely 700 years ago, a group of proto-enterprising brokers in Antwerp announced an increase in the price of wool. They justified it to the weavers with a concoction about an infestation of sheep ked, across the Channel, in the large English flocks whose fleece the brokers sold. Prices were up in London, they lied, and anyway cash was required to enlarge local, Low Country, wool production capacity. It was a matter of developing self-sufficiency. A few new ewes were needed. If the proposed price change was accepted immediately, the brokers continued slyly, they could all count on an inexpensive, reliable supply for the future. Otherwise, looms would lie idle.

As a matter of fact, between 1280 and 1310, wool prices rose from seven to 17 livres per sack. Those brokers had simply invented a shortage in order to bump up and perpetuate their own already inflated profits.

Another phrase which came out of the Antwerp affair, incidentally, is 'to pull the wool over someone's eyes'.

Mrs. Kocajowski closed her umbrella and walked over to the Non Fiction section. From the 800's she took a book of short stories.

"Is this real or make believe?" she asked. The librarian looked at it and answered, "make believe."

Mrs. Kocajowski headed back for the shelves. "I can't read make believe," she said, "it's too confusing; it always seems so real and then I don't know what's what. It's not safe."

After a few minutes she brought two 920's, biographies, to the librarian. One was a fictionalized Joan of Arc, the other an old Life of Theodore Roosevelt. "This one's not real, this one is," said the librarian.

Mrs. Kocajowski started out the door with the Life of Theodore Roosevelt. "Excuse me," said the librarian, "I didn't check that out yet."

Mrs. Kocajowski put the book on the counter. While the librarian stamped the due date, Mrs. Kocajowski ruefully remarked, "I'm always in a hurry, I don't know why. I've got nowhere to go. It's as if I did have, but I don't."

Having taken the book, Mrs. Kocajowski turned, opened her umbrella and left. At the door, she had to close the umbrella to get through.

Recommended Reading

UNFIT FOR HUMAN CONSUMPTION / David G. Maillu
Nairobi, Kenya : Comb Books, 1973. Six shillings

This is a popular novel, set in Nairobi, about civil servant Jonathan Kinama, a high liver who fights and fucks a lot and gets in plenty of trouble. His paycheck is stolen. Then his wife shows up from the village and berates him in public for non-support. He loses his job. Finally, he kills himself.

The book seems to be telling young men to steer clear of hot sex and booze.

But we should think twice before concluding anything about something from such a faraway place.

By the way, this 93-page paperback measures just $5\frac{1}{8}$" by $3\frac{5}{8}$". The bright color photos on the front cover were taken by the author.

According to the back cover, David G. Maillu "writes frankly, like the average African elder, without undue sensitivity in his use of language."

Actually, and all kidding aside, Maillu's use of English isn't only frank, it's also unpredictable, provocative, funny, free, and inspiring. I'd give an eye tooth to have thought up this sentence:

"As he crossed Government Road arguing within himself whether or not to go back to the office, an Alfa Romeo car screeched hard to his side and he jumped high up with automation like a Masai."

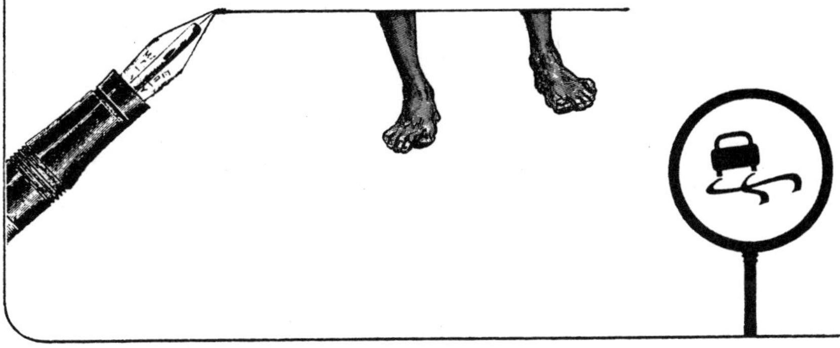

Shilling by shilling, Daphne saved enough from her job at the shebeen to buy a Sanyo model X-810 twin cassette portable stereo.

She used to tape shows off the radio, for playback with coffee before work, so her head, and her shoulders, and her hips would be wide awake.

When she figured out how, she started mixing her own. Her favorites were the old girl groups like Dark City Sisters and The Flying Jazz Queens, but she also enjoyed The Jabulani Quads, The T. V. Sisters, Michael Jackson, The Cockerels, and any group with Mister King Jerroo.

Meanwhile, the government was constantly forcing them out of the townships, out to the bantustans, to live with and like scrawny trees. They made Daphne go to a remote corner of Kwa Zulu where dead babies far outnumber C batteries, and it almost broke her spirit.

THE IMMIGRANT WORKER

I'd sung 'Solidarity Forever' at demonstrations back home but it wasn't until our wildcat walkout at the cabinet shop that I really understood.

Malcolm, Toots, Mike, and I were the work crew in a slightly shady shop, underground in fact, in the basement of a building across the road from the World's End pub.

We were sanding down scruffy old furniture and refinishing it for sale as antiques. My special job, since I was smallest and least able to handle the heavy pot-sander, was disguising the spots of wood-filler which were revealed when the old paint was sanded off. Using a fine brush and powdered tints and oil, I was covering the spots with fake grain and wood-knots, and since I'm color-blind

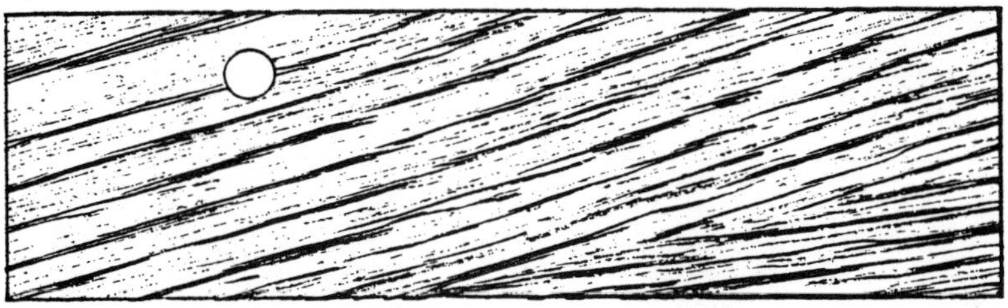

I must've been making some strange knots, but that's being beside the point.

Working conditions were being lousy. Pay was being good, however, and unreported to the powers that were being. Everything would've been ok if not for smarmy Howard, our supervisor, who'd been a labourer, like us, before being promoted.

One Friday, close to quitting time, after we were already cleaned up and changed and anticipating our week's end pint together, Howard ordered us to stay late and unload a lorry just in from Wales.

Fuck off, we said. No YOU fuck off! he yelled right in my face since I was smallest. YOU're fuckin fired!

I was feeling shock and shaking, I think. Feeling alien. Alone. What force on earth is weaker than the feeble force of one?

But the union makes us strong. Straight away, Mike was quitting. Then Malcolm too. Then even Toots. We'll wait for our wages across in the pub, we said.

Two hours later we were still waiting, wondering what to do, when the big boss came walking in, sitting down, apologising, asking us to be back at work on Monday, and handing us our envelopes, which included a raise seeing as how he wouldn't be having to pay that dope Howard anymore.

MORAL HAZARD

There are occupational hazards in every walk of life. Homemakers, for instance, face three kinds of hazard: physical hazard, psychogenetic hazard, and moral hazard.

Physical hazard is easy to picture.

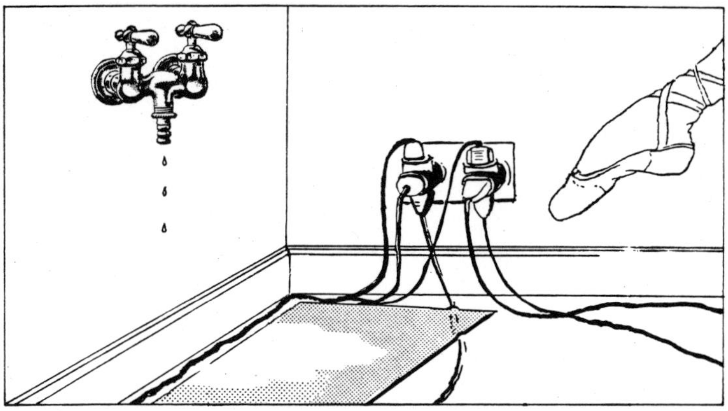

Psychogenetic hazard, less easy, takes many forms. To illustrate, let's look at a typical homemaker's projections on the theme of intrusion, because intrusion is a preoccupation of some significance in this particular occupation.

Louise G., homemaker, age 31, one child, working husband, seven-room duplex house, Hoover canister-type vacuum, etc.

Every day, Louise G. faces conflicting sorts of intrusion fantasies, i.e. there may be welcome or unwelcome intrusions. There may be neighborly intrusions, postal intrusions, giggling infantile intrusions, and, now and then, timely intrusions. On the other hand, there may be spooky intrusions, sudden loud intrusions, and, worst of all, forcible intrusions.

So much double meaning encourages emotional disequilibrium. This is the number one psychogenetic hazard in homemaking.

Resilient homemakers develop defenses. Louise G. carries her purse with her, even while vacuuming, and she always keeps her passport in it.

The main moral hazard in homemaking, meanwhile, is the unhealthy potential for tyranny in matters sanitary and nutritional.

A SANATORIUM

An unsigned article in LA CONSTRUCTION MODERNE, July 22, 1899, page 509, translated from the French.

Everyone knows that the latest treatments for tuberculosis involve going for a rest cure in an environment full of fresh air, and free from dust and germs.

Sanatoria have been built, therefore, in the mountains, in the snow, and patients are expected to live out of doors as much as possible, and to sleep with the windows open.

Mr. Hannotin has begun work on a mountain sanatorium and, aside from giving it an innovative and interesting design, he has had the idea of constructing it using the most modern building materials, such as reinforced concrete.

In the first place, this is an exceedingly economical material, but it has the added advantage of being moldable. That is, it can take various forms and, thanks to it, one can create rounded rooms which, having neither angles nor corners to collect dust, would be easy to sanitize with a simple hosing-down.

In the epileptic's apartment, everything is padded shag, of a single, quiet, fall color. Outsized walnut sculptures, which resemble brains, hang high on the walls. A dim light glows around a row of easy anti-convulsant pill dispensers, in case there's warning time. In case the incapacitating pills are swallowed, the refrigerator's stocked for a few days. Speaking of time, there's a clock on the wall, as well as a Wechsler Adult Intelligence Test, to measure post- and inter-ictal alertness. Near the clock, a barometer almost cheerfully implies the possibility of prediction. And manufacturers' labels, evidence of known origins, dangle from the furniture. Other epileptics come here to relax.

THE TRANSMISSION OF DADA
Robert Motherwell wrote that Josef Albers told how Kurt Schwitters used to tell a hilarious story about a parrot with a hernia, but Albers couldn't remember how the story went.

" Some of the most interesting experiences I had on my trip to the other side of the world were experiences I didn't think I had." ~*Richard Foreman*

When we went overland from Izmir to India in 1970, we had to learn to live with very little privacy. We stayed in cheap hotels where the toilet was down the hall. On the streets, we were watched and followed. Once, in Pakistan, it really got to us.

We were waiting for a train in Lahore, sitting on a bench, our packs between our knees, and the temperature over a hundred. Slowly, a crowd of young men gathered, until there were fifteen or so, in a semi-circle around us. We were curiosities, and they were curious. But poor, very poor. They had grown up against tremendous odds, the biggest of which was poverty. They just stood and stared at us. It got kind of scary. Finally Mary turned to the nearest guy and asked, "Do you speak English?" He gestured yes.

"Look," she said, "we're people too, just like you. It's uncomfortable with all of you standing around staring at us." The guy said something in Punjabi to the others, and they all melted away.

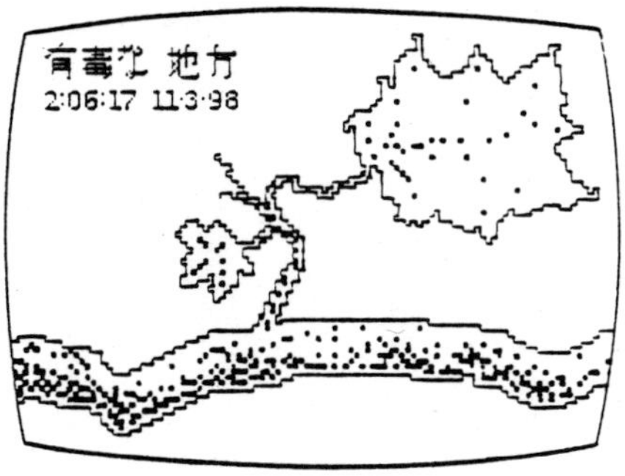

In Massachusetts, Tabi-Jido the substi-tourist turned toward one of the few remaining sugar maples and transmitted its image to Toku Fubito, abed, in Nagasaki.

NO 9346.

Greetings from sunny South Florida! Stupid nightlife and drug rub-outs. Mall architecture and complicated racism. And ostentation. On Worth Avenue in Palm Beach some rich bitch won't think twice about shelling out 40 bucks for a few pounds of imported Jamaican coffee. She won't think even once about the imported Jamaican sugar-cane cutters 40 miles away in Glades County, slash and burn all day, breaking their backs so she can sweeten her brew. "Eventually," as an Everglades trail sign says, "the death-hug of the strangler fig will prevail here."

PARLIAMENT
BUILDINGS

M. Kasper
106 High St.
Florence, Mass.

Dear Constituent,

As you probably know, I have consistently voted in favor of next to nothing. This month, a big bill, having to do with social policy, is somewhere in the legislature. How this bill drones through committee, and the style with which it slouches into and around our highest chamber are of the utmost import. The future of urbanity is at stake.

I've passed some pretty sleepless nights lately, wondering how to vote. But yesterday, watching television, I found guidance. I saw how all the existing brands of aspirin, because they derive from the same active ingredient, do the same middling job of headache relief. And that's how it is with lawmaking in this country. You see, citizens, given our headaches, and given the single interest served by the alternate remedies, it doesn't matter how I vote. So you can rest easy.

God bless,
The Hon. Pell Mell, Senator

In the Sixties, the Vietnam War was terrible. I left the States. So I was in Afghanistan when I got my letter.

FEDERAL BUREAU OF INVESTIGATION
UNITED STATES DEPARTMENT OF JUSTICE

The U.S. Attorney has informed me that you have been reported delinquent by Local Selective Service Board 24-A for failure to report for induction.

Failure to obey instructions of your Local Board may subject you to prosecution in the U.S. District Court.

I would appreciate if you would contact me at LE 5-7700, Extension 230, between 8:00 am and 5:00 pm in order that arrangements can be made to clear up your delinquency.

Walter Ver Steeg
Special Agent - FBI

(Not that he waited around for phone calls.)

Then came the Seventies. After the American defeat in Vietnam, conscription faded away, and I came home. Agent Ver Steeg was probably filing interstate traffic tickets, or something.

Then the Eighties. The goddam business patriots demanded more war, and got several. The Draft Boards re-formed.

Wake up Walter, you worm!

UPRIVER (A 'Keats and Chapman' story, in the manner of Flann O'Brien)

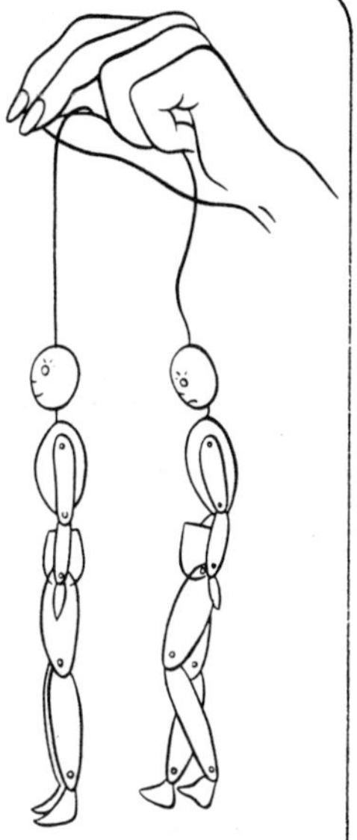

During the Vietnam War, Keats and Chapman worked for a time in Saigon as stringers for the net-works. Once, they got wind of a secret visit nearby by Ho Chi Minh and they set off to interview him, upriver by rowboat.

Along the banks, everything was devastated. It was groundwork for decades of deprivation. There weren't even birds in the trees. Where were the birds? Instead, now and again, natives shouted stuff from the shore, but Keats and Chapman couldn't make out what.

The air around was at least as hot as inside them, and, since there were no birds, insects had taken it over, and the crosscurrents grew so strong Keats and Chapman were constantly grasping at oars yanked out of their cradles.

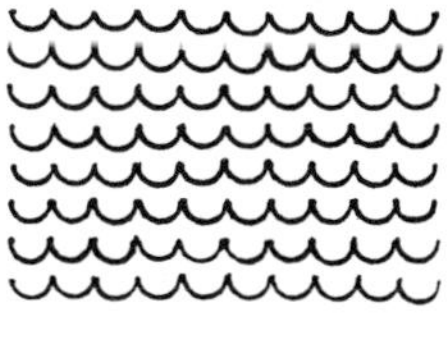

"Whew," remarked Keats, mopping up, "it's a hard row to Ho," where-at Chapman toppled overboard.

"Heedlessness, greed, and other self-indulgences," he said, "these are typical features of behavior nowadays. And I display my share. What matters most is how I feel. Well, yes," he conceded, "sometimes for a moment I'm ashamed. When? Afterwards. For example, when at last I sense that by driving my supermarket shopping cart so recklessly I terrified an old woman in a wheelchair . . . or that I acted like a scavenger in the house of a friend's dead father last week . . . or that my public confessions (say, this one) tend to be bumptious and ambitious.

"These are random recent examples," he said. Later he said, "But even pangs of conscience, for me, are slightly delicious. What matters most is that I feel. No," he went on, "I don't think that this is moral idiocy. It pains me to think there's such a thing at all as moral idiocy."

In 1952, as usual, the poor got poorer. "Defense" spending, at 50,000 megabucks, dominated the federal budget. Twenty-six corporations reported sales in excess of one billion dollars. Inflation snatched our purses.

In 1952, the Dormanton, New England city fathers, half-noticing an increase in the number of hungry old faces on Main Street, authorized the construction of a municipal housing project in a remote, ill-serviced section of town. It wasn't until 1973, when the mini-mall was built and a grocery moved in, that food was within walking distance of the project. By then the population of the project was mainly Puerto Rican.

One of the city fathers who approved the building permit for the mall, a certain candy bar salesman, promptly became the mall's first tenant. His was the grocery store. It still is. What's more, he was elected mayor last year. And today, September 22, 1978, when I compared prices in the mayor's grocery with those in one of the local supermarkets (none of which are on or near bus routes), this is what I found:

Product	Mayor's store	Supermart
Milk, 1 gallon	$1.69	$1.45
Eggs, large, 1 doz.	.95	.93
Fleischmann's margarine, 1 lb.	1.13	.99
Skippy peanut butter, 18 oz.	1.35	1.15
Domino sugar, 2 lbs.	.95	.75
Maxwell House coffee, 1 lb.	3.49	2.59
Cheerios, 20 oz.	1.59	1.29
Ronzoni elbow macaroni, 1 lb.	.65	.51

Time — The Breath of Investment

What with two jobs and 54 hours a week working, my wide-wale corduroys were wearing thin, so I reached in my wallet and what did I find? No time for shopping, that's what! Whereupon, one lunch break, I went to Citibank for a loan.

My credit line was weak, but they ushered me into the Board Room for a chat anyway. There they sat, the so-called *direct interlocking directorate*. First thing, I took a photo with my hidden camera (thus, in small ways and spare moments, I try to make propaganda).

From left, front row: George P. Jenkins (representing Bethlehem Steel), Frank Barnet (Union Pacific), Harry J. Gray (Aetna Insurance), John D. deButts (A T & T), Edward Lewis Palmer (Del Monte); second row: Amory Houghton Jr. (Dow Corning, and IBM), Lord Aldington (Lloyds Bank), Eleanor H.B. Sheldon (Rand Corporation), two unidentified Feds, Clifton C. Garvin (Exxon), Robert S. Hatfield (General Motors, and Eastman Kodak), Walter Wriston (General Electric); back row: Peter McColough (Xerox), Harold J. Haynes (Boeing), Lawrence Fouraker (N B C).

I begged to borrow four hours a week, for a year, any old terms. They said they'd decided to restrict Citibank's customer base to bigwigs. Besides, the prime rate was rising, they said, and borrowed time, though it might be a boon today, would be a burden tomorrow. In short, they showed me the door.

I'm lucky all I got was a simple no. What with their connections, one or more of those tycoons could've put the squeeze on one or both of my bosses. I'm lucky I didn't get mandatory overtime.

THE ANESTHESIA OF INFLATION

When they get sick, commodities develop proportional relations, one to another. They become exchangeable quantities.
Over the years, this unsound system alchemizes gold. But gold wears down as it circulates, so, where money is most subject to wear, where it circulates rapidly, substitute metals come to symbolize gold.
Then, at last, after a long long wait in line, having memorized every advertised interest rate and savings plan, we receive from an underpaid teller some intrinsically worthless paper, our weekly withdrawal.

INVERSE

OBVERSE

Dog poop! What we need now is to rid society, as soon as possible, of the dropsy of paper currency with which it's inflated.

FADING

A NEW ASPECT

Millie's view of Shangri-la was blocked. The child-support payments had stopped because she'd been dating Eddie, and now Eddie had moved to Milwaukee. Little Sammy kept pointing his finger at her, making aggressive noises. The Welfare Office was insisting she leave the kid at some basement daycare and look for gainful employment. In her eyes (gone gray lately, from green) one could see shame, self-pity, dejection, disorder, fatigue, fear, desire, and loneliness. And here it was, Thursday night of all nights, and the TV was blinking !

"Don't fiddle with your knobs !" a voice in the box ordered, "Your set's o.k. It's our error. We'll fix it." "No," said Millie, "It's my fault." Then, slowly, the screen went dark, leaving just a pinhole of light through which she wished her head might fit, but loosely.

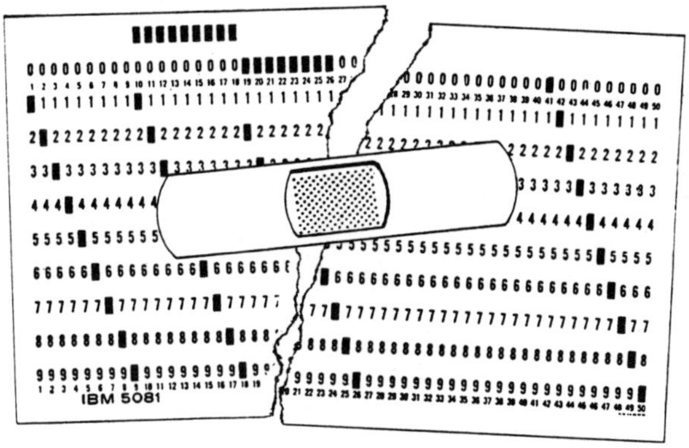

A DIGEST OF THE LAWS

Finally it became apparent: this liberal keynote speaker was proposing that each government insert into its hierarchy a new lower echelon to interface with disgruntled petitioners.
After the speech there was polite applause. Then the convention of functionaries rose onto tired feet from hard chairs.
"Long live the Civil Service!" they shouted. "Long live Nation-Statism! Long live the First, Second, and Third Worlds!"
Their cheers floated up into the Great Dome of the Great Hall, which, due to a structural flaw, was supported mainly, and barely, on the basis of the political-moral condition of the functionaries. Cracks everywhere, patched with red tape.

When at last the Dome fell in, naturally, the functionaries had long since filed out. Only the janitorial staff was affected.
One widow went to the appropriate assistant functionary to apply for compensation. She was told that the middle functionary she needed to see was tied up at a meeting, planning the next convention, but his decision would be mailed to her.

Years ago, in 1921, Alexandra Kollontai wrote: "Some third person decides your fate. This is the whole essence of bureaucracy."

HUMAN NATURE NOT YET REMADE - A PLAY

(The curtain rises in a Kremlin parlor, May 1920)

In Act One, it's morning and many people begin to come to sympathize with Lenin on the non-party terrorist's attempt on his very life. The Chief narrates to them how the whole thing happened. It's complicated. Around noon, he winds up with a weary chuckle and a few words from *State and Revolution*. "After all, and all the same," he says, "it's more pleasant and useful to live through a revolution than to describe it." Pleasant ?!

The Ukrainians in the parlor, who've felt the lash of four armies in three years, disagree but hold their tongues. Perhaps they'll get a few lines in Act Two.

The Chief instructs the balalaika players to begin to supply music and they start to pound their balalaikas. The Chief provides refreshment for everybody. Those who arranged the terrorist attempt are among those dancing in the parlor to celebrate the Chief's safety.

(This whole act lasts for about eight hours.)

SYSTEM ALL RUN DOWN
A Detective Fiction

1.

When Inspector Fitzly and Sergeant Trim arrived, the deputy minister's body had already been removed from the boudoir. Fitzly was relieved, Trim a trifle crestfallen. What clues there were were put in plastic bags:

- a typewritten statement from the assassins, full of the usual leftwing drivel and promise of more mayhem;
- a shell casing;
- some threads disengaged from a broken window.

But no finger prints, and no witnesses.

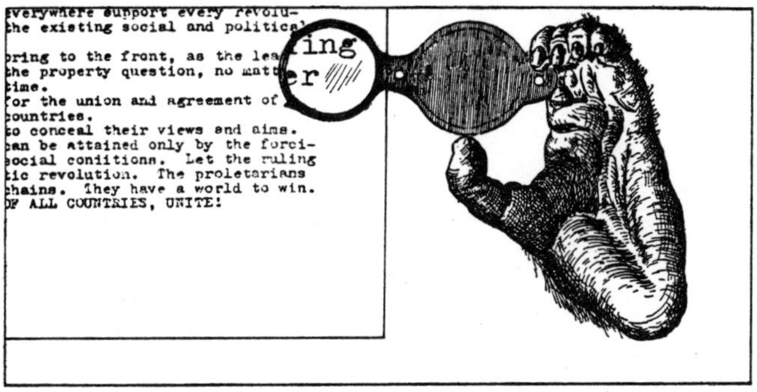

2.

The typewriter turned out to be an Olivetti Lettera 22 with several wonky characters; the paper was a common 22 lb. bond. The casing came from an untraceable .22. So Fitzly phoned down to the numerology lab. Then he phoned upstairs to enquire if manpower was available to examine every typewriter in London. Then there was a knock at the door.

3.

"Come in."

"I'm Dwiggins, Internal Affairs...You'd best come quietly, sir ... Trim's in custody... 22 bloody burglaries, you two!... He's told all. Forget that murder case. You're suspended."

NURSE HARRIS MOPS UP: A TRUE STORY

One.

Nurse Andy Harris gently closed the door to Ann Harrod's room and went across to the nurse's station. It was the end of his shift. Ann's marriage proposal was certainly something to think about! All that money!

As he slipped his coat on, Andy could see Dr. Harrison waiting for him down the hall. She was with her brother and her brother's wife. Tonight they were all going to Chez Alphonse for dinner. Andy wished he could decipher Dr. Harrison's real feelings for him. She was so attractive, but so obscure.

He was interrupted in the midst of his reverie by a buzz from Room 506. Oh darn that old Mr. Hardin! On his way to answer the call, Andy shot an inviting glance at Dr. Harrison. Oh darn! Hardin had done it again! Lately the old, dying man had no control over his bowels. All over the bed!

Andy threw up his hands. "Look at this mess!" he yowled. "C'mere everybody! Look at this mess!" Dr. Harrison, her brother, and her brother's wife came and stood at the door. Andy pulled Mr. Hardin off his bed and sat him on the toilet. "Stay there 'til you're done!" he said firmly. Then he stripped the smelly sheets and got towels for the floor.

Once, he had to go out of the room for more towels. He noticed Dr. Harrison sneaking into Ann Harrod's room. "That's odd," he thought.

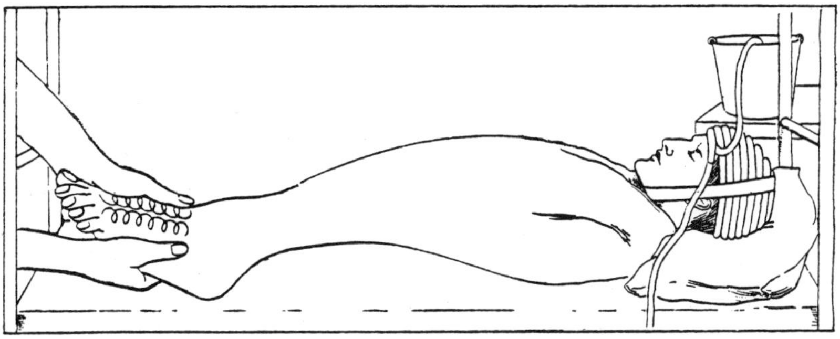

Two.

The next day, Mrs. Hardin came to see her husband. His breakfast hadn't been touched. "Angela," he said, "I felt so ashamed. I don't want it to happen again." He died that night.

Lately, a feeling—over and above that of simply being beaten—of being fooled, by the powers that be, into being accessories to the worst sorts of crimes—again—the feeling is growing. We try to resist their exceptionally subtle powers of deception, but we're growing older, which is part of another growing social problem: every year, the number of people over the age of 65 in the U.S. is rapidly expanding. There are more and more infirm older people, year after year, more and more. But fewer nurses. Whereas in Nicaragua, the number of nurses is rising, even though older Americans account for only 3% of the population there, compared with 8% in the U.S.

Lately, some U.S. older people—some ethically infirm ones in particular—liars mostly—have been posing as politicians and snitching privileges from the populace—intent, especially, on killing off Nicaraguans before they grow old—maintaining the statistical edge—because they're afraid that if U.S. voters find out that there are more nurses AND more older people in Nicaragua, we'll grow restive. The whole thing makes one sick. I asked an older woman with whom I work every other month putting out a newsletter for the local Council on Aging if she was sick too, and she said yes.

Why New Yorkers Leave Home

This is a substantially true story and I'll tell it straight, as it was told to me by an older man who's opinionated, yes, but honest and not at all senile.

It was New York City, in Autumn 1929, just after the Crash. Jim, having no fixed address and no moola, used to spend nights in the subway. A lot of poor people did it. And among them there was a code of honor. According to the code, the younger, relatively healthy ones rode on the trains at night. They curled up in corners, with the noise, the windows that wouldn't close (especially on the El), and the cops at every terminal. The long benches on station platforms were reserved for older people, so they could stretch out and approximate a real snooze. Then, one day, an army of carpenters invaded the stations. On orders from some big shot, they put dividers on the benches, so people couldn't stretch out. I asked Jim what the older people had done then, but he didn't know. By the way, if there's another collapse, next year for instance, where will we go? And presuming we find a place, are the present-day authorities any more likely to let us sleep?

Since my brother's been living and working in the imperial capital, he's become a somewhat different person, or so it seems to me. I guess the differences between us are a lot like those that generally make it hard for the provinces (where I live) and the capital to understand one another.

My brother was telling me how he judges the people he meets. First thing, he says, he tests them with an imaginary test. He imagines himself entering a room... they turn toward him from the other side... He suddenly tosses them a volleyball!
Maybe they bobble it.
That fails.

But it's so controlling, I say, and it's all about performing ...about athletic performing, of all things! The values, I say... but I'm so appalled, I can't find the words to finish.

Well, he says.

... the war's been going on for years and years, overlapping with its aftermath till you can't tell which is which ... Those who've survived live in dereliction. They use the leftover kerosene cookstove as a vase for plastic roses, or rather for green plastic stems, with little green stumps where plastic leaves and flowers once fit ...

On occasion, they eat rotten fruit ; more often they have hunger headaches. And lice, and arthritis ... They make believe they're communicating, but they express themselves in over-complicated ways, or mumble, or move into the next room ... the burnt-out one ... so someone following can't quite hear ...

MAXIMS

The rich is a victim of prior styles of life, and movies, much less than the poor are.

The poor, especially when old, chew and chew though their mouths are perforce empty.

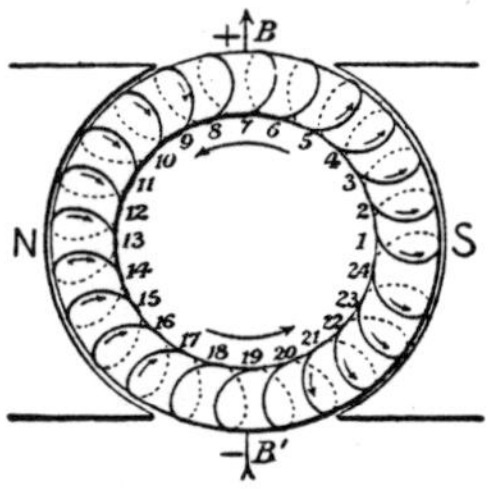

The rich is dressy to the point of being untrustworthy.

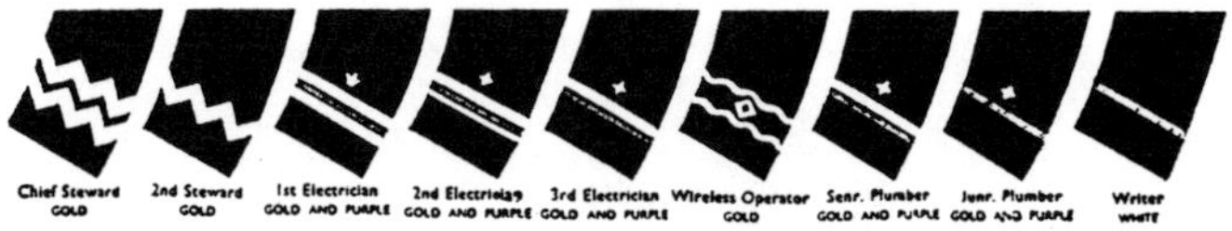

The poor have so far been luckily saved, but they know quite well the way to disaster.

The rich never steps aside.

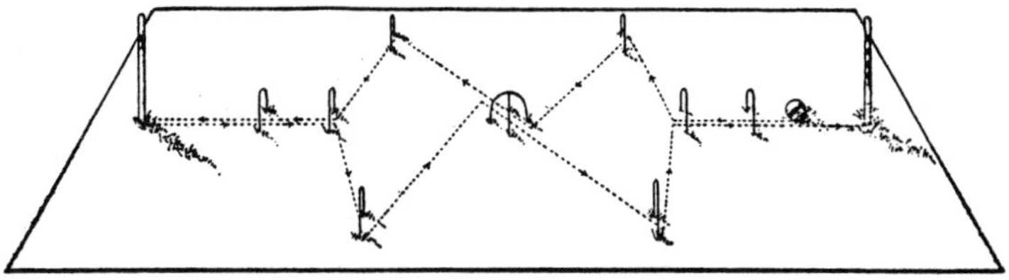

The poor generally get their electricity by tapping illegally into power lines.

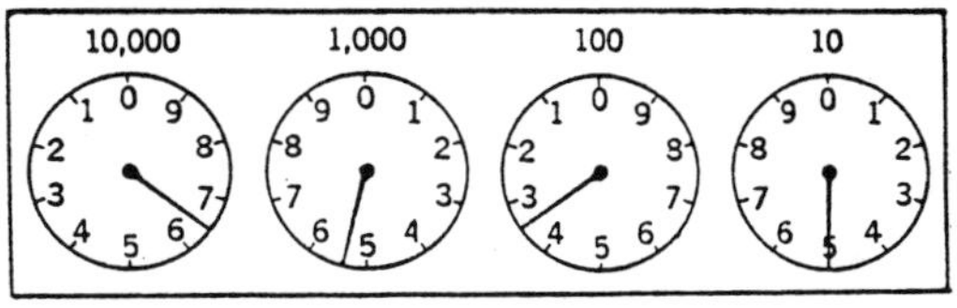

The rich rests easy, on the backs of the poor, soft from flogging.

Hey Joe!

Joe's nerve's not what it once was. It's the unemployment. When he first noticed the unemployment, about six months ago, Joe didn't take much notice. But the thing persisted, and then it enlarged. Symptoms like dyspepsia, insomnia, systemic grumpiness, and a dull green wishful thinking turned up. Last month eleven of Joe's letters of application were returned unopened. He stopped seeing friends. The unemployment started cruising up and down his spine in an alarmingly casual and sinister fashion. Institutionalization was unavoidable.

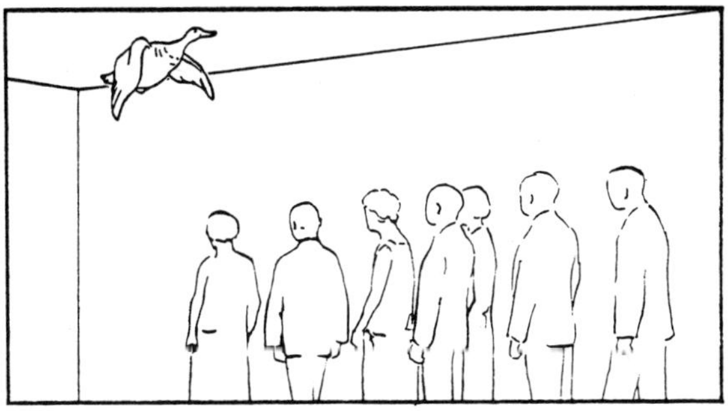

They watch Joe now. Every two weeks, if he can prove he's still got the unemployment, he gets a handful of maintenance pills. So that's why Joe's nerve's not what it once was.

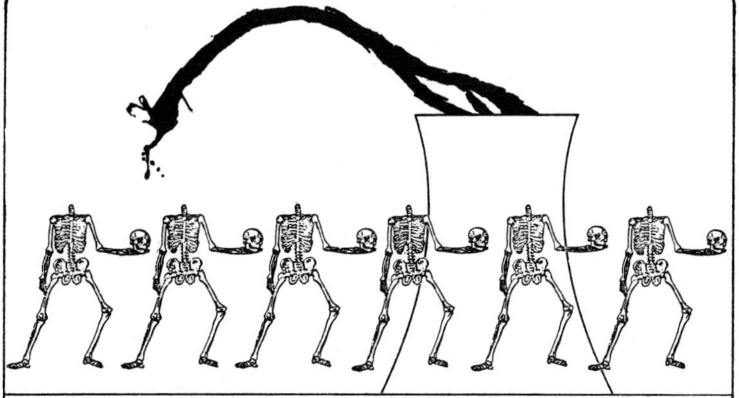

The Life History Scanner was first tested in an autopsy dated April 9, 1997. The decedent was 50 years old. Cause of death was called thyroid cancer. The Scanner successfully traced the cancer to a dose of isotopic iodine ingested by the decedent at a party in Dormanton, New England, between 9 and 11 p.m., on July 7, 1979.

Across the room, the decedent's spouse was engaged in an obviously amorous conversation; jealousy drove the decedent to gluttony. But that's beside the point. The point is that what the decedent gobbled was a quantity of bite-sized Hershey chocolates.

For three months prior to this episode, in and around the Hershey factory in Dauphin County, Pennsylvania, radiation levels had soared. First an 'accident' at a nuclear power plant, and then some unannounced foul-ups during the clean-up. Hershey bars were loaded with contaminated ingredients.

According to the Scanner, the decedent also absorbed radiation from other products manufactured in the same vicinity: Pennsylvania Dutch Egg Noodles, Pepsi-Cola bottled in Harrisburg, Sico kerosene, Kinney shoes, Purina Cat Chow, Equanil tranquilizers, etc.

Regrets

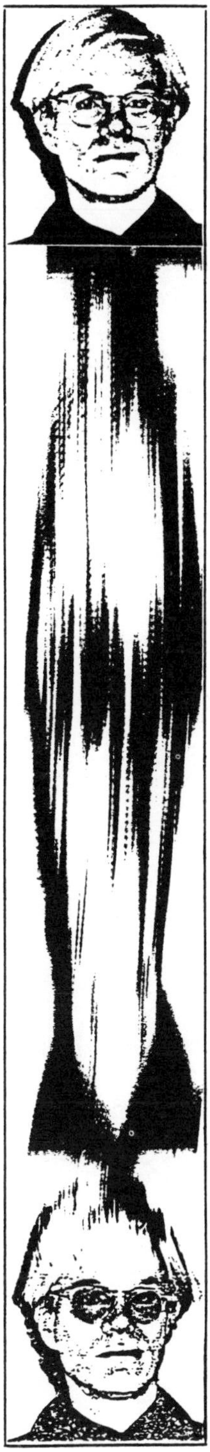

It's a bummer that Andy Warhol was only 58 when he died a few years ago. I was 21 the time I met him, in Denver, in early 1968.

I was visiting for three weeks with my friend Richard Myers. One afternoon we did some mescaline so as to be stoned for a showing of shorts by Warhol - with an appearance by him and Viva Superstar afterwards - that evening at the University.

Half an hour into the movies we felt an urge for a cigarette in the next room so we slipped away.

Into a brightly lit little cafeteria, closed for the day, feeling very empty, with some chairs upended on tables, other chairs pulled up to tables... at one of which sat... Andy Warhol! And Viva was pacing back and forth along a side wall.

Trying to be cool and unobtrusive, we sidled over to a corner and lit cigarettes. But Warhol invited us to join him. "Whadya think of minimal art?" he asked when we sat down across the table.

I'd never seen such a pasty face, such acrylic skin. I was tongue-tied at first. I can hardly remember. Then, though, he turned out to be easy to talk to, friendly, curious when he learned I was just back from six months in Turkey. After a bit he asked if I wanted to be in a picture he was filming south of Denver someplace. Viva was still pacing, ignoring us. I explained that I'd been drafted and needed to get out of the country; how much would I get paid? He smiled and shook his head, "just room and board." Maybe, too, I was slightly scared. I'm sorry, I said. He said, "me too."

In the auditorium later, Warhol wore shades and never said a word. Viva fielded all the questions, some hostile. I've never seen anybody faster on their feet in front of an audience.

Now she and I are the only ones still alive... Oh Richard! Wasn't Viva smart that night! And I dumb! To have missed the chance to be in 'Lonesome Cowboys', with Taylor Mead, my favorite actor!

Many thousands of people died in Ethiopia in what the living people there called 1968.
We called that year 1976* but little matter.
Around here, 1968 was an average year in a romantic decade. Where were we then, Mary ?
Eating. Same as now.

* In Islam, it was 1396. Nestorians called it 2287, and Jews 5736. Only those in, well, privileged positions, could simultaneously inhabit all the places where these different calendars are honored. Furthermore, that would be time travel, and their sense of past and future could be compromised. The disorientation and estrangement around here are stupefying. It's hard to swallow. As Walter Benjamin said, "Things get stranger every century."

Gregory and Stan regularly ride the bus to work together. Usually, Gregory does most of the talking. Lately, he's been preoccupied. His job runs out in June and new jobs are scarce. The other day though, he changed the subject to Teddy Bears.

(Bus stop. Three new passengers.)

It turns out Gregory is one of the nation's leading authorities on Teddy Bears. "What figure in this century," he asked Stan, "what figure, real or imagined, is so unambiguous a symbol of comfort as the Teddy Bear?" Stan couldn't think of a single one.

(Stop. Six high school kids off at the back.)

Gregory showed Stan a letter from Bruce Bleery. Bleery, Gregory explained, is a businessman who operates a chain of Teddy Bear collectors' dens, and he puts out a magazine called "Paw Prints."

(Stop. Two off, two on, and the bus idles awhile.)

The letter was postmarked Honolulu. Even though Bleery lives in Washington D.C., all his mail is routed through a radio station he owns in Hawaii. According to Bleery, that's because he doesn't trust the San Francisco Post Office. Stan nodded. He too had known many strange characters who worked there.

(Stop. Three off, two on.)

In the letter, Bleery offered to publish Gregory's research. Stan noticed that the letter's closing was: "Friendly grrrrs,
(signed) Bruce Bleery, Bearo No. 1."

(Stop. One on.)

Gregory wants Bleery to set up a Teddy Bear museum, with Gregory as curator. When they got off the bus, Gregory was telling Stan he wouldn't have any trouble building a collection. Lots of older people, rather than take their Teddy Bears to the grave, would give them to a museum.

Fred's on a creeper under the chassis struggling to unbolt a broken clamp from the goddam exhaust pipe. His fingers barely fit around the goddam speedometer cable to where the bolt's rusted stuck, much less the wrench. He's tried every lubricant on the goddam market. He's exhausted. He's goddam frantic. Then he hears a voice from inside the engine. "I want a knuckle." "What?" says Fred. "I want a knuckle," it repeats. Suddenly the wrench jerks and Fred jams his knuckle and wham!!! the bolt comes loose.

I should've realized she'd be dangerous when

she told me how, when she was a kid, when her mother showed her a picture, in a book, of lions eating Christians in a Roman stadium, she burst out crying, and when her mother asked why, she pointed to one lion and whimpered, "Look, this one hasn't got a Christian."

PSALM 23

Unit A. Sheep.

1. "The LORD is my shepherd; I shall not want."
   Discuss the appearance of sheep.

2. "He maketh me to lie down in green pastures."
   Describe the supplies needed by a flock of sheep.

3. "He restoreth my soul; he leadeth me..."
   Is leading any better than following?

Unit B. Shepherd.

1. "Thy rod and thy staff they comfort me."
   Make an organizational chart of his staff.

2. "Thou preparest a table before me."
   What makes a perfect host? Tell students the story of Lot and the angels, Genesis 19.

3. "I will dwell in the house of the LORD forever."
   Show a videotape of the interior.

Patron Saint of AIDS

AIDS sufferers say, "Lord help us."

The Archbishop of Genoa says, "AIDS is a punishment from God."

The Pope says, "Homosexuality is a moral disorder."

The Jesuits (ever devious?) say, "Pray to St. Aloysius Gonzaga, who nursed the sick in the sixteenth century, our pick for patron saint of AIDS."

St. Aloysius Gonzaga, after El Greco

This Gonzaga (research reveals) said, "I am a piece of twisted iron; I entered religion to get twisted straight."

And Jesus said, "What man is there of you, whom if his son ask bread, will he give him a stone?"

He was always so proud
of his penmanship. His
signature, with its lovely
stutter and swoop, was
almost Arabic.
Now, Mom says, he can't
sign his name anymore.
Those elegant, ever so leg-
ible block capitals which
he used for crossword
puzzles and mailing labels,
when he was able, used to
start sketchy, then grow
bold.
His face is so thin now.
I hold his thin hand in
mine. We squeeze.
He's given me his faith
in handwriting.

Casually exuberant,
Chuang Tzu, Taoist, strolls.
Stops. Stoops. Spots a rock.
Picks up & examines. Lobs.
Shielding eyes to watch.
Yikes! Smack dab into bird!
Emperor's favorite nightingale!
Plummeting..Thud! "You'll roast for that,"
remarks Hui Tzu, companion. (Wise men can't stand
such companions.) "Ah bitter," Chuang Tzu snivels &
avers, "Inadvertent! Just one of those things!"
"Not so fast!" retorts Emperor, Confucian. "Those who blame
fate to get off some hook, we sentence to hang from another."

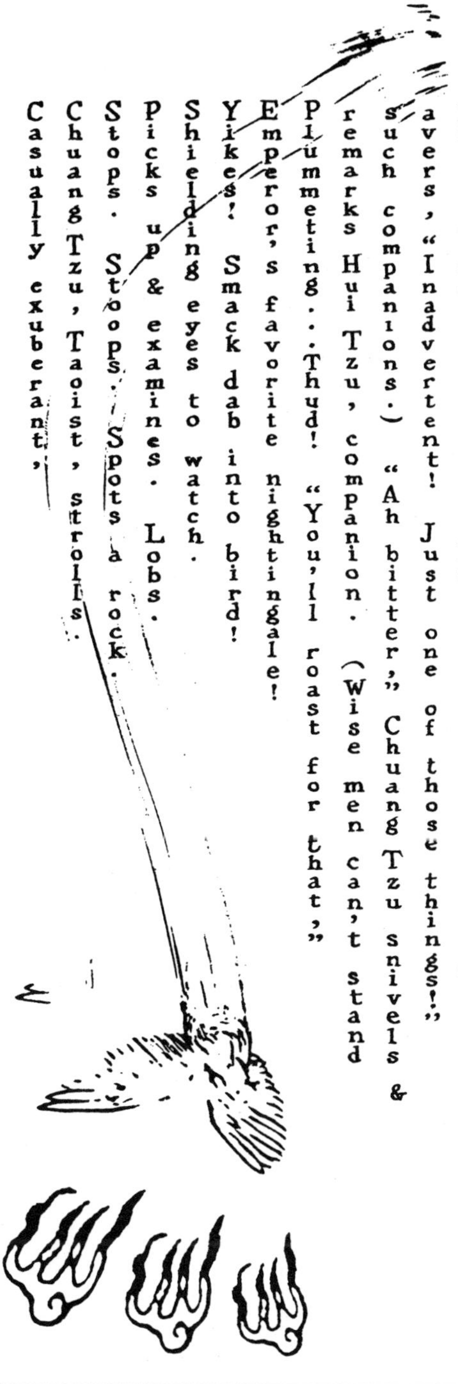

HIGH-GRADE OUTINGS UNDER A POPULAR SYSTEM

Compound sentence: *Travel and you possess the world.*

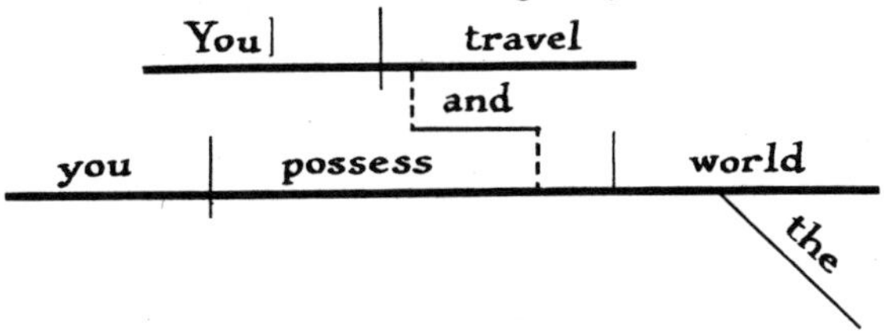

Explanation:

Since the independent clauses which make up any compound sentence are of equal rank, each one is indicated by a heavy line. *To possess*, for instance, has various meanings.
The direct object *world* is separated from its verb by a short line drawn at right angles to the main line. By the way, historically, there have been countless fruitless discussions on the subject of objectifying the world. Only transitive verbs, of course, can take an object in this manner.
In any case, no one who's ever travelled from Bombay to Benares in a third class rail car onto which, at one stop, a madman, bound and screaming, was dragged for transport to an institution, would dare say they in any sense possess the world.

Surrounded with injustice and guilty of complicity, we sometimes get confused about what to do.

Take Jane. She considered it immoral to feed pets when people were starving - in Africa, for instance - so she killed her cat.

Other books by M. Kasper
who was born – 1947 – and partially educated
in the Bronx, and now lives
in western Massachusetts,
include "Border Crossing" 1973;
"Chinese English Sentence Cards" 1979;
"Odds n Ends From The Lost n Found Department" 1980;
"Billy! Turn Down That TV!" 1983
"Verbo-Visuals" 1985
"Plans for the Night" 1987